SCIENCE A

THE CAVE OF SHADOWS

Explore light and use science to survive

Richard and Louise Spilsbury

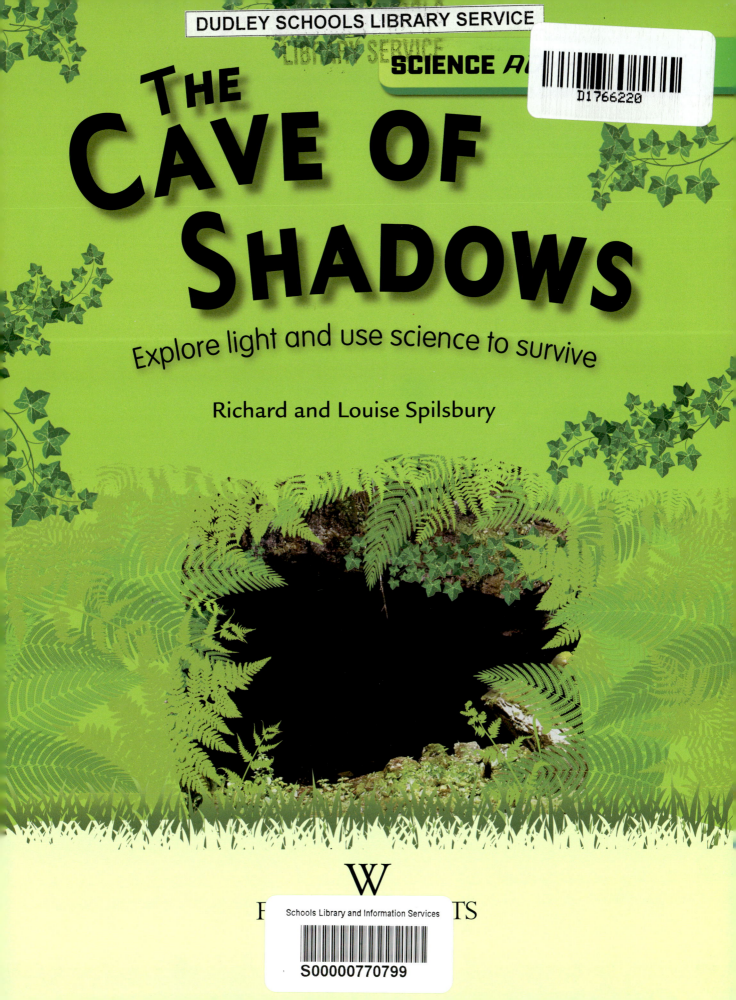

W

First published in 2013 by
Franklin Watts
338 Euston Road
London NW1 3BH

Franklin Watts Australia
Level 17/207 Kent Street
Sydney NSW 2000

Produced for Franklin Watts by
White-Thomson Publishing
+44 (0)843 208 7460
www.wtpub.co.uk

Series concept and editor: Alice Harman
Series consultant: Penny Coltman
Designers: Alix Wood and Samantha Richiardi
Experiment and character artworks: Stefan Chabluk

A CIP catalogue record for this book is available from
the British Library.

HB ISBN: 978 1 4451 2302 8
Library ebook ISBN: 978 1 4451 2593 0
Dewey Classification: 535

Picture Credits
Dreamstime: Anton Petuhkov, Berean, Sifis Diamantidis, Sylwia
Nowik, Tetyana Kysyonz; Shutterstock: Ales Liska, andreiuc88,
Andre Nantel, Archiwiz, basel101568, Devochka i zaicheg,
dramaj, Dziurek, elsyl, fotofundi, fototehnik, Galyana Andrushko,
geographio, jeff gynane, Kurt Kleeman, malko, nubephoto, Potapov
Alexander, romawka, RUI FERREIRA, Sergemi, spline_x.

Every attempt has been made to clear copyright. Should there
be any inadvertent omissions, please apply to the publisher
for rectification.

Printed in China

Franklin Watts is a division of Hachette Children's Books,
an Hachette UK Company.

www.hachette.co.uk

Bold words in the text are included in the glossary

WHO'S WHO?

JESS

Jess is a bit of a daredevil. She's always first to try something new. She loves skateboarding, climbing and adventure stories.

BEN

Ben is a bit of a kit monster. He carries his rucksack with him at all times and it's full of useful – and not so useful – stuff.

AMELIE

Amelie is a science whizz. She's not a know-it-all, but she often has the right answers. She isn't too keen on getting her clothes dirty and her hair messed up.

ZAC

Zac is the youngest and although he never wants to be left out, he can get a bit nervous and is easily spooked.

CONTENTS

Into the dark   6

We're not alone   8

The long tunnel   10

Seeing spooks   12

Monster of the cave?   14

Glinting in the dark   16

Finding treasure   18

Hidden spaces   20

Found but lost!   22

Into the light   24

Quiz   26

Find out more   28

Glossary   29

Index   30

INTO THE DARK

'He-e-e-lp!' shouts Jess. 'Come quickly! Poppy's chased a rat into this cave.'

'I told you not to bring that puppy with us!' snaps Amelie.

'Well, I'm not going into that dark, scary cave after her. Let's wait till she comes out,' says Zac.

'She could get hurt or lost! Come on, we'll see all right once our eyes get used to the dark,' pleads Jess.

'No,' says Amelie. 'Without a light we won't be able to properly see where we're going, and it could be dangerous.'

A loud yelp comes from inside the cave and the three friends look at each other in panic. Just then, Ben runs up – with his bulging rucksack on his back, as usual.

'It's okay,' Ben says quickly. 'I've got a torch and a headtorch. Let's go.'

'I've got a bad feeling about this...' warns Zac, following the others into the dark.

WHAT DO YOU THINK?

Is Amelie right? If there is no light, can you see?

6

PROVE IT!

Test how light helps us to see.
You need:

- bag made from thick, tightly woven material
- a few small objects such as a ball, a pencil, a spoon (nothing sharp)
- small torch (not too strong a light)

①

Put a few small objects into your bag.

②

Rest the bag on the table, and look into it. Hold the top edge tightly around your eyes, so that no light can get in from outside. What do you see?

③

Turn on the torch and hold it so that it points into the bag. What do you see? Turn off the torch so that it no longer gives out light. What happens now?

WHY IT WORKS

Amelie is right, we need light in order to see. We see some objects because they are luminous (they give off their own light), such as the Sun or a torch. We see other objects when light shines on them and bounces into our eyes. That's why we can only see the objects in the bag when the light from the torch bounces off them and back to our eyes.

WE'RE NOT ALONE

'Good job you had those torches in your bag, Ben,' says Zac. 'It's so dark in here we really wouldn't be able to see a thing without them.'

'Wait!' whispers Jess urgently, holding her hand up in warning to the others. 'I think there's someone or something else down here…'

'There can't be,' says Amelie. 'Poppy would have barked at them. Keep moving – it's really cramped here.'

'Hang on,' says Ben. 'Shine your torch ahead again.'

'No! What if it sees us?' hisses Zac. 'Then we'll all be in real trouble.'

'I don't think so,' laughs Ben. 'Jess, you were scared by your own **reflection** in that pile of scrap metal over there!'

'Well, how come there aren't reflections of me all over the walls, too?' retorts Jess, a little embarrassed. 'And what kind of idiot dumps their rubbish like that?'

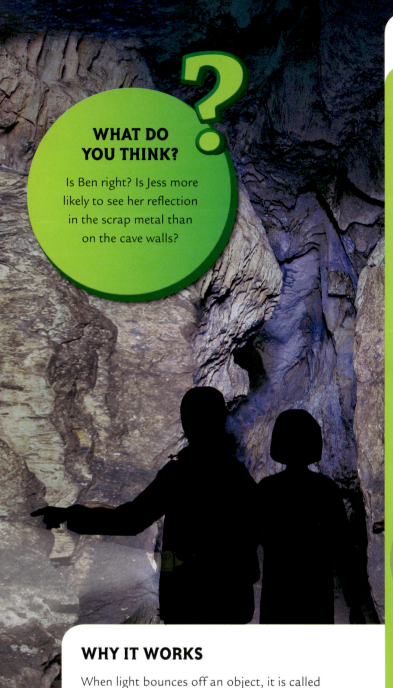

WHAT DO YOU THINK?

Is Ben right? Is Jess more likely to see her reflection in the scrap metal than on the cave walls?

PROVE IT!

Test how different surfaces reflect light. You need:

- scissors ● ruler ● piece of A4 card
- modelling clay ● torch ● white paper
- fabric ● sandpaper ● small mirror
- crinkly aluminium foil

1 Ask an adult to help you cut a thin slot about 5 cm long and about 5 mm wide in the middle of one of the edges of the card. Use the modelling clay to stand the card upright on a table, with the slot at the bottom.

2 Close the curtains or turn off the light so the room is a bit darker. Lie the torch on the table so it shines through the slot in the card. One at a time, hold the paper, fabric, sandpaper and crinkly aluminium foil in the narrow beam of light coming through the slit. What do you notice?

3 Now hold a mirror in the beam of light. What do you notice?

WHY IT WORKS

When light bounces off an object, it is called reflection. Different surfaces reflect light differently. When light hits a very smooth and shiny surface, such as a mirror, it reflects at a matching **angle** – like a ball bouncing off the ground. When it hits a surface that is rough, the light bounces off in all sorts of directions so no clear image can be seen. This is like bouncing a ball on very uneven ground. There are some surfaces from which light does not bounce back at all, and no reflection is seen.

THE LONG TUNNEL

'Hurry up!' snaps Jess. 'I can hear Poppy barking up ahead, she might be hurt.'

'I can't go any faster,' says Amelie. 'It's too dark back here.'

'Aaa-aa-r-g-h!!' screams Zac. 'I've fallen and something's got me by the foot. Get it off. Get it off!'

'Hang on,' says Ben, shining his torch at Zac. 'You haven't been grabbed by a hungry cave monster – your foot is just trapped between two rocks!'

'Well I can't see where I'm going because you two are hogging the torches,' complains Zac.

'It's not our fault,' protest Jess and Ben together. 'Light travels in a straight line.'

'Yeah, that's a likely story,' mutters Zac.

WHAT DO YOU THINK?

Are Jess and Ben right?
Does light travel in
a straight line?

PROVE IT!

Test how light moves.
You need:

- four pieces of card (all the same size)
- torch ● pencil ● ruler
- drinking straw ● modelling clay

1 Draw a cross on three of the cards by laying a ruler from one corner to the other across both diagonals. Use the pointy end of the pencil to make a hole in the middle of each of these three cards (where the X meets in the middle). Wiggle the pencil around a bit to make the hole big enough to poke the straw through.

2 Use the straw to line up the three holes on the cards. Then use modelling clay to hold the cards in position on the table, with the holes lined up. Remove the straw. Use modelling clay to stand the fourth card (with no hole) behind the third card. Shine a torch through the hole in the first card. What happens?

WHY IT WORKS

Jess and Ben are right. Light is a form of **energy** that travels in straight lines called **rays** from light **sources**. When the three holes on the cards are lined up, the light travels through the holes. If the middle card is moved to one side so that the holes are not lined up, the light ray doesn't pass through the hole in the middle card. It travels in a straight line and hits the middle card to one side of the hole.

3 Now move the second card in the row and reattach it to the table so that it doesn't line up with the others. Shine a torch through the hole in the first card. What happens?

SEEING SPOOKS

'Come on, Zac,' says Amelie. 'We're going to fall behind the others.'

'I'm not going another step,' whispers Zac, pointing with a shaking finger at a large pale shape glowing in the tunnel ahead of them.

'It lo-loo-looks like some sort of cave ghost!' splutters Amelie. 'What do we do?'

'Let me think... stand here and tremble? Or cry?' suggests Zac.

'Hang on a minute,' sighs Amelie. 'I know what it is now – it's just a **column** of **translucent** rock! It looks like it's glowing because only some of the light from Ben's torch is getting through it. Phew!'

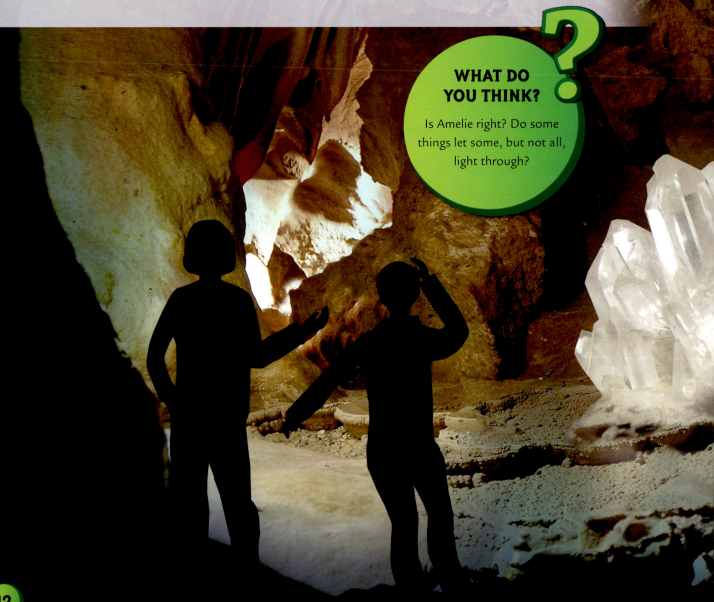

WHAT DO YOU THINK?

Is Amelie right? Do some things let some, but not all, light through?

PROVE IT!

Build a tester tube to find out what can happen when light hits different objects.
You need:

- six cardboard tubes ● scissors
- six elastic bands
- six different materials, such as cling film, greaseproof paper, plastic shopping bag, aluminium foil, white paper, coloured paper, fabric

1 Cut 10 cm squares out of your different test materials.

2 Wrap one square of material round one end of each cardboard tube. Hold each square in place with an elastic band.

3 Take it in turns to hold the open end of each tester tube to an eye, and point the other end at a window or light and look through it. (Don't point your tester tube up towards the Sun or a very bright light, as this could hurt your eye.) How much light gets through?

WHY IT WORKS

When light hits a material, three things can happen. If the material is **transparent**, like clear flat glass, light passes through it easily and we can see clearly through it. If the material is translucent, like a net curtain, it lets some light through but we cannot see clearly through it. Compare a bathroom window to the ones in your classroom. How are they different? If the materal is **opaque**, like wood, it blocks light completely so we can't see through it at all.

MONSTER OF THE CAVE?

'Now what?!' snaps Jess. 'Why are you pulling at my sleeve, Zac?'

'Keep still. I think there's a giant bat up ahead of us.'

'A bat?' screams Jess. 'No, I hate those things! It'll get tangled in my hair and suck my blood!'

'Those are just silly stories,' says Ben crossly. 'Bats are too clever at finding their way in darkness to get tangled in anything. And they eat fruit or insects, not people – even if your blood would taste sweet from all the cake you eat!'

'Cool it, all of you! It's just a **shadow** from a moth on the front of Ben's torch.' says Amelie.

'What, the biggest moth of all time?! I'm not waiting to find out if you're right this time,' says Jess, unconvinced. 'Let's run – we still haven't found Poppy!'

WHAT DO YOU THINK?

Is Amelie right? Can a small object make a big shadow?

PROVE IT!

Test how light makes large and small shadows.
You need:

● torch with a strong light **beam**
● darkened room
● three small objects for making shadows, such as a comb, feather and toy dinosaur

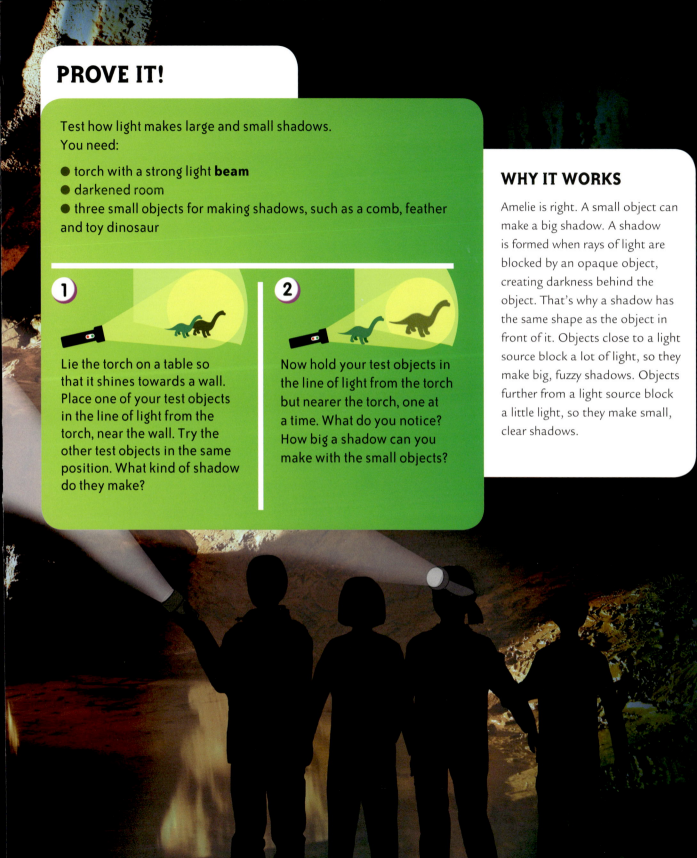

1 Lie the torch on a table so that it shines towards a wall. Place one of your test objects in the line of light from the torch, near the wall. Try the other test objects in the same position. What kind of shadow do they make?

2 Now hold your test objects in the line of light from the torch but nearer the torch, one at a time. What do you notice? How big a shadow can you make with the small objects?

WHY IT WORKS

Amelie is right. A small object can make a big shadow. A shadow is formed when rays of light are blocked by an opaque object, creating darkness behind the object. That's why a shadow has the same shape as the object in front of it. Objects close to a light source block a lot of light, so they make big, fuzzy shadows. Objects further from a light source block a little light, so they make small, clear shadows.

GLINTING IN THE DARK

'What are you doing?' cries Ben, grabbing Jess to stop her reaching into a pool of water.

'Let go! I'm trying to get that thing **glinting** in the water. If it's Poppy's name tag, we'll know she went this way and not down the other tunnel.'

'But the water might be deeper than it looks, and you could fall in.'

'Don't be daft,' says Jess crossly. 'I've got great eyesight – I can see how deep it is.'

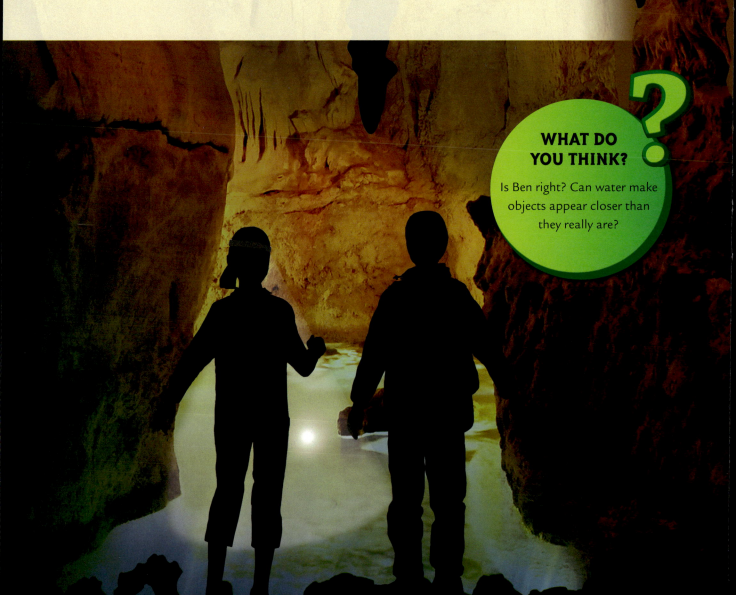

WHAT DO YOU THINK?

Is Ben right? Can water make objects appear closer than they really are?

PROVE IT!

Try this water trick.
You need:

● coin ● mug ● jug of water

2

Keep your head still, and with one hand slowly pour water into the mug. Does the coin come back into sight?

1

Place the empty mug on a table and drop a coin into it. Look over the rim of the mug so that you can see the coin, and then move the mug slowly away from you until the coin just disappears from sight.

WHY IT WORKS

Ben is right. Water bends light, so when you look at objects under the water they can appear closer than they really are. This happens because light travels at different **speeds** through different **materials**. Light slows down when it moves from air to water, and as it slows down it changes its **direction**. This bending of light is called **refraction**.

'OK, you were right,' admits Jess. 'The water was deeper than it looked, and you had to hold my legs so I could reach into it safely.'

'Yeah, but you were right, too,' says Ben kindly. 'It was Poppy's name tag, so we know we're on the right trail!'

FINDING TREASURE

'Yeeurgh!' shouts Amelie with disgust. 'A huge rat just ran across my feet into that hole!'

'A rat?!' shrieks Zac, leaping into Jess's arms. 'Are there more of them?'

'No,' says Jess, trying to drop Zac to the floor as he clings on tight.

'Maybe Poppy went through that hole, too,' says Ben, crouching down. 'Wow! There are coloured gems in here. I could buy some fantastic kit for my rucksack if we can get them out!'

'Sorry to disappoint you, but those are just worthless rock **crystals**. They're acting like a **prism** and splitting your torchlight into its different colours,' explains Amelie.

'Can you say that again in English, please?' asks Ben, looking confused.

WHAT DO YOU THINK?

Is Amelie right? Can light be split up into different colours?

PROVE IT!

See if you can separate light into different colours. You need:

- A4 white card ● scissors ● shallow baking tray
- water ● modelling clay ● small mirror ● ruler
- window with sunshine coming through it

1 Cut a 10 cm long, 2 mm wide slit into the long edge of the card, a few cm in from the edge.

2 Put about 2.5 cm of water in the bottom of the baking tray. Then rest the small mirror in the tray at an angle, with the top edge resting against the side of the tray. Use blobs of modelling clay to hold the mirror in place.

3 Place the water tray in front of a sunny window, with the mirror facing the window. Hold the card so that light shines through the slit onto the part of the mirror under the water. Keep moving the card until the mirror reflects light back onto the card. What can you see?

WHY IT WORKS

You have made a water prism. A prism is something that can split light into its separate colours. Amelie is right. Light seems colourless but it is really a mixture of colours. We can see the colours of light when it shines through a prism of glass or crystal. When light shines through drops of rainwater, we sometimes see a rainbow.

HIDDEN SPACES

'Now what?' groans Jess. 'Poppy is small enough to get through that gap, but we're not. How can we check if she went that way?'

'Zac's got a small head. Perhaps he could poke it through the hole,' suggests Amelie helpfully.

'Oi! What a cheek!' says Zac. 'My head may be on the small side, but my brain is big enough to work out that I'd get stuck trying that.'

'Rucksack to the rescue!' shouts Ben. 'I've got all we need to make a periscope – lucky you guys drank all the juice and left me with the cartons! I'll chuck this glowstick up first, and then use a periscope to bend the light and see what's in there.'

WHAT DO YOU THINK?

Is Ben right? Can a periscope help you see what's on the other side of a solid wall?

PROVE IT!

Try making this simple periscope.
You need:

- two empty one-litre rectangular milk or juice cartons
- double-sided sticky tape
- two mirrors that fit into the cartons ● card ● scissors

③

① window

Open the top of one carton and the bottom of the other. Tape the open parts together to make one long box. Now ask an adult to help you cut two windows out of the box – one on each side. One window should be at the top of the box's front side, and the other should be at the bottom of its back side.

②

Ask an adult to help you make diagonal (45-degree angle) slits in the top and bottom of each of the wider sides of the carton. The slits must be at the same angle and position on each side of the carton, in the middle of the sides.

Use double-sided sticky tape to stick each mirror to a piece of card that will slide through the slits. The reflective sides of the mirrors should face towards the two windows. Look through the bottom window. You should be able to see out of the top window. If you can't, adjust the mirrors until you can. Then try looking around a corner with your periscope!

WHY IT WORKS

Ben's right. A periscope uses mirrors to change the direction of light and help you see around solid objects. Light reflects away from a mirror at the same angle that it hits a mirror. In a periscope, two mirrors are angled so that light from outside hits the top mirror and reflects to the bottom mirror. This light reflects into your eye, so you can see the image from the top mirror.

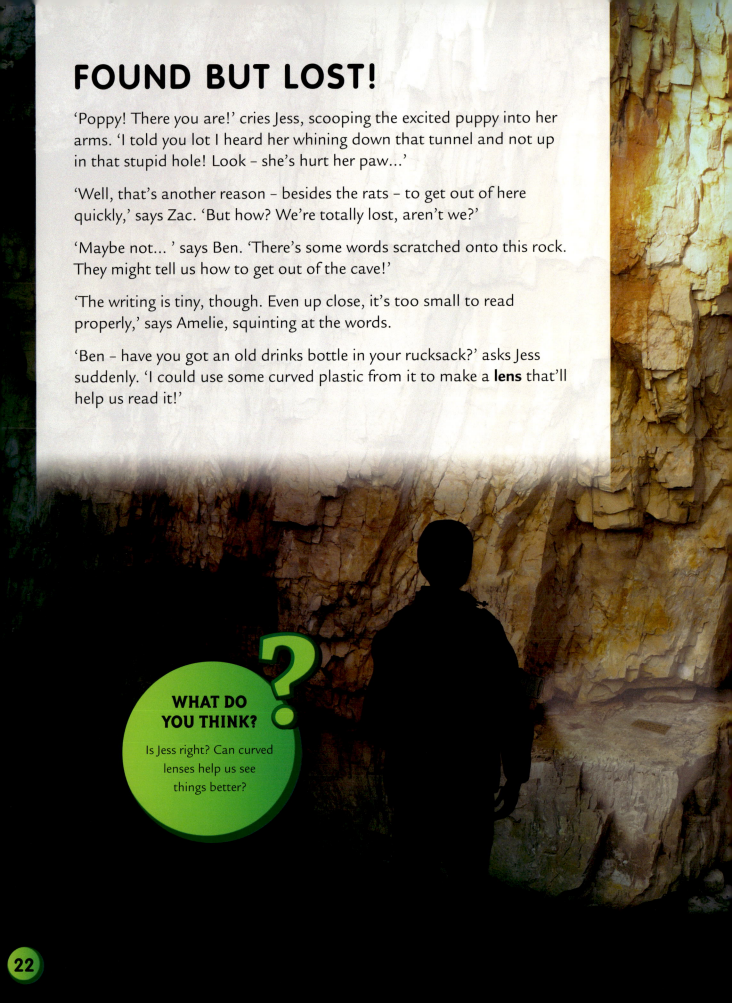

FOUND BUT LOST!

'Poppy! There you are!' cries Jess, scooping the excited puppy into her arms. 'I told you lot I heard her whining down that tunnel and not up in that stupid hole! Look – she's hurt her paw…'

'Well, that's another reason – besides the rats – to get out of here quickly,' says Zac. 'But how? We're totally lost, aren't we?'

'Maybe not… ' says Ben. 'There's some words scratched onto this rock. They might tell us how to get out of the cave!'

'The writing is tiny, though. Even up close, it's too small to read properly,' says Amelie, squinting at the words.

'Ben – have you got an old drinks bottle in your rucksack?' asks Jess suddenly. 'I could use some curved plastic from it to make a **lens** that'll help us read it!'

WHAT DO YOU THINK?

Is Jess right? Can curved lenses help us see things better?

PROVE IT!

Make and test your own **magnifying** lens.
You need:

- empty two-litre drinks bottle ● water ● scissors
- marker pen ● book or newspaper

1

Use the marker pen to draw a circle at the top of the bottle.

2

Ask an adult to help you cut out the circle. Then lie it on the table so it makes a bowl shape, and put a large drop of water in the middle of the disc.

3

You have made a water prism. A prism is something that can split light into its separate colours. Light is made up of colours. It really is! When it shines through drops of water, we get a rainbow, and we can see colours of light when it shines through a prism of glass or crystals.

Hold your magnifying lens over the words in a book to see if it works.

WHY IT WORKS

Jess is right. Lenses are curved pieces of transparent plastic or glass that refract, or bend, light. Magnifying lenses use **convex** lenses, which have at least one curved surface and are thicker in the middle than at the sides. Your plastic bottle lens and the top of the water drop both curve outwards, so you have created a double convex lens. When you hold the lens close to a page, it bends and widens the light rays before they reach your eyes, making the words appear larger.

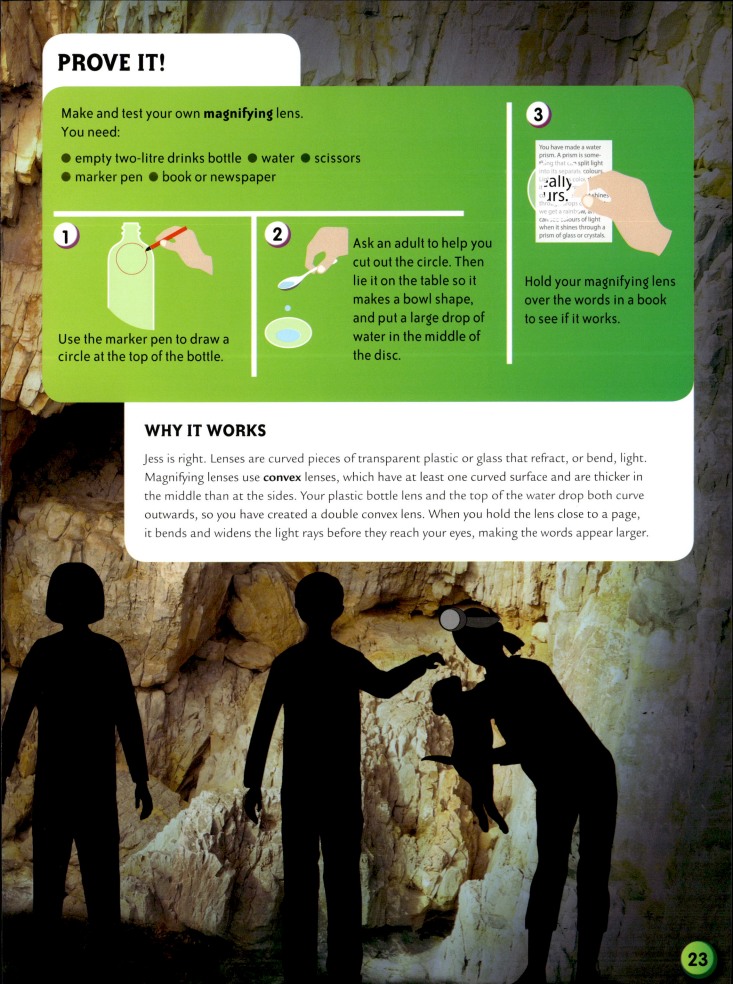

INTO THE LIGHT

'We made it! I thought we were never going to get out of there…' says Jess. 'Good job the magnifying lens worked and the writing told us which way to go. It was pretty confusing even with the directions.'

'Ow!' cries Ben suddenly. 'After so long in the dark, it hurts my eyes to go into the bright sunlight.'

'Me too,' say Zac and Amelie together, shielding their eyes with their hands.

'But we need to get Poppy home fast to clean her paw and check it's okay,' says Jess.

'Well, you might not believe it but I can solve this problem!' says Zac proudly. 'I did a project on **Inuit** people recently. They wore **goggles** with slits in to protect their eyes from the sunlight **glaring** off the snow. If Ben's got duct tape in his rucksack I can make us some.'

'What does Ben not have in that rucksack?' laughs Amelie. 'Let's make them and get home!'

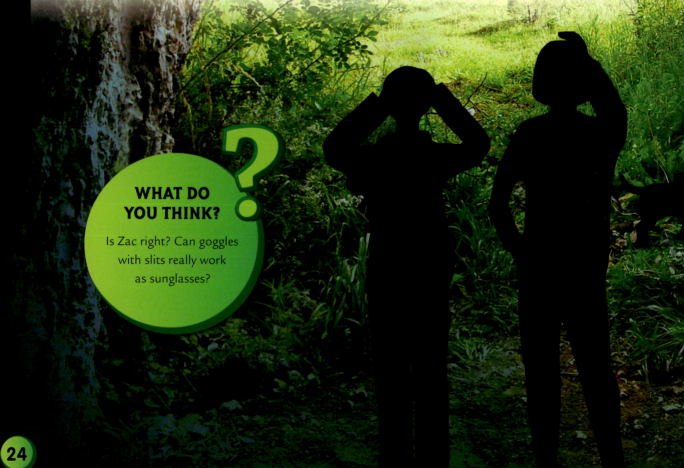

WHAT DO YOU THINK?

Is Zac right? Can goggles with slits really work as sunglasses?

PROVE IT!

Make your own goggles.
You need:

- string ● scissors ● duct tape (or other wide tape)
- paper clip ● marker pen

1

Wrap a piece of string around your head at forehead level, and cut one end where the string meets. Then cut two pieces of duct tape just a bit longer than the string and stick the two sticky sides of the pieces together. Line the two sides up carefully before sticking them together because they are tough to pull apart again!

2

Bend the duct tape strip into a circle, and clip the two ends together with the paper clip. Put this mask on over your eyes. Use the marker pen to very gently draw a line where your eyes are.

3

Take the mask off and cut lines where the marker pen lines are, to make two slits. When you put the goggles back on, make sure they fit close to your face to prevent light getting through.

WHY IT WORKS

When light shines into your eyes, it hits a part called the **retina** at the back of each eye. The retina sends messages about what your eyes see to the brain. Bright sunlight can damage retinas. These sunglasses let in enough light for your eyes to see, but the opaque material stops too much sunlight entering and hurting your eyes.

QUIZ

1 Objects that give off their own light are called:

a) luminous

b) reflective

c) transparent

2 When light bounces back off an object or surface, this is called:

a) bending

b) absorption

c) reflection

3 How do you see the words on this page?

a) Light reflects off the book and enters your eyes.

b) Light reflects off your eyes and enters the book.

c) Light comes from your eyes and reflects off the book.

4 Which of these three surfaces reflect the most light?

a) rough and dull

b) smooth and shiny

c) smooth and dull

5 Which of these statements are true?

a) Light travels in straight lines.

b) Light travels through any material.

c) Light is a form of energy.

6 Match each word with its meaning.

a) transparent

b) translucent

c) opaque

1) lets some light through but we cannot see clearly through it

2) blocks light completely so we can't see through it at all

3) light passes through it easily and we can see clearly through it

7b | 8b | 9a | 10b | 11a | 12c How did you do?

7 When do shadows occur?

a) When light reflects off a shiny surface.

b) When an opaque object blocks the path of light.

c) When light travels through an object.

8 When light bends as it passes through water we say it…

a) reflects

b) refracts

c) bounces

10 When light hits a mirror, does it…

a) get absorbed by the mirror

b) reflect away at the same angle that it hits the mirror

c) reflect away at many different angles from the mirror?

9 What does a prism do?

a) It splits light into its separate colours.

b) It gives off light.

c) It creates shadows.

12 Which part of the eye can be damaged by sunlight?

a) eyelashes

b) eyebrows

c) retina

11 What are lenses?

a) curved pieces of transparent plastic or glass that refract light

b) curved pieces of opaque plastic or glass that refract light

c) curved pieces of transparent plastic or glass that absorb light

FIND OUT MORE

BOOKS

Glaring Light and Other Eye-burning Rays (Disgusting and Dreadful Science)
Anna Claybourne, Franklin Watts, 2013

Hands-on Science: Sound and Light
Sarah Angliss, Kingfisher, 2013

*Light and Sound (*Sci-Hi*)*
Eve Hartman & Wendy Meshbesher, Raintree, 2010

Light and Sound (Essential Physical Science)
Louise & Richard Spilsbury, Raintree, 2014

The Illuminating World of Light (Graphic Science)
Emily Sohn, Raintree, 2010

WEBSITES

Learn about light, and how we use it to see and be seen:
www.3m.co.uk/intl/uk/3mstreetwise/pupils-need-light-to-see.htm

Click on the 'Light' section to read, play games and revise ideas about light:
www.bbc.co.uk/bitesize/ks2/science/physical_processes

Find out more about how eyes work:
www.childrensuniversity.manchester.ac.uk/interactives/science/brainandsenses/eye

Watch this video about the reflection and absortion of light:
www.bbc.co.uk/learningzone/clips/absorption-and-reflection-of-light/242.html

Every effort has been made by the publisher to ensure that these websites contain no inappropriate or offensive material. However, because of the nature of the Internet, it is impossible to guarantee that the content of these sites will not be altered. We strongly advise that Internet access is supervised by a responsible adult.

GLOSSARY

angle shape made by two lines that meet at the same point

beam narrow strip of light

column tall, straight, solid piece of rock

convex shape that curves or bulges outwards

crystal special three-dimensional solid with flat sides and a regular shape

direction the way in which something or someone travels or faces

energy force or power

glare when light is so strong that it makes it difficult to see

glint when something reflects light and quickly flashes

goggles special glasses worn to protect the eyes

Inuit native people who live in parts of North America and Greenland

lens curved glass or plastic that makes things look bigger/smaller/clearer

magnify to make things appear bigger

material type of substance

opaque something you cannot see through

prism something that separates light into its different colours

ray narrow line or beam of light

reflection light or an image that is bounced back off a surface

refraction the bending of light

retina part at the back of the eye that sends messages to the brain

shadow dark image on a surface, caused by an object blocking light rays

source where something first comes from

speed how far something moves in a given amount of time

translucent something that lets some, but not all, light through

transparent something that you can see through

INDEX

A

air 17
angle 9, 21

B

bend 17, 20, 23

C

colour 18, 19
crystal 18, 19

D

dark 6, 8, 10, 11, 14, 15, 24
direction 9, 17, 21

E

energy 11
eye 6, 7, 16, 21, 23, 24, 25

G

glass 13, 19, 23
glow 12, 20
goggles 24, 25

I

image 9, 21

L

lens 22, 23, 24
light 6, 7, 9, 10, 12, 15, 18,
   20, 21, 23, 24, 25

M

magnify 23, 24
materials 13, 17
metal 8, 9
mirror 9, 19, 21

O

opaque 13, 15, 25

P

periscope 20, 21
plastic 22, 23
prism 18, 19

R

ray 11, 15, 23
reflection 8, 9, 19, 21
refraction 17, 20, 21, 23
retina 25
rock 10, 12, 18, 22

S

shadow 14, 15
shine 7, 8, 11, 15, 19, 25
speed 17
Sun, the 7, 13, 19, 24, 25
sunglasses 24, 25
surface 9, 23

T

torch 6, 7, 8, 10, 12, 14, 18
translucent 12, 13
transparent 13, 23
tunnel 10, 12, 16, 22

W

water 16, 17, 19, 23
wood 13